# Polly and the Piano

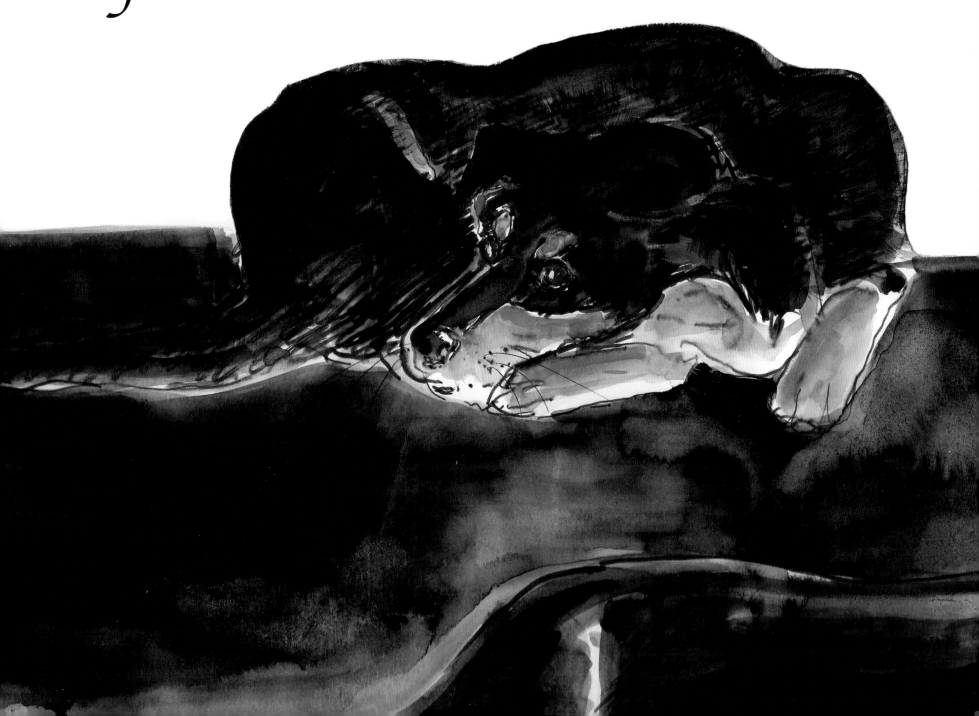

**Also by Carol Montparker**

*The Blue Piano and Other Stories*
*A Pianist's Landscape*
*The Anatomy of a New York Debut Recital*

# Polly and the Piano

*Story & Paintings by*

## Carol Montparker

**Amadeus Press**

Pompton Plains, NJ • Cambridge, UK

Published in 2004 by

Amadeus Press, LLC
512 Newark Pompton Turnpike
Pompton Plains, New Jersey 07444
U.S.A.

Amadeus Press
2 Station Road
Swavesey
Cambridge CB4 5QJ, U.K.

For sales, please contact
NORTH AMERICA

UNITED KINGDOM AND EUROPE

AMADEUS PRESS, LLC
c/o Hal Leonard Corp.
7777 West Bluemound Road
Milwaukee, Wisconsin 53213 U.S.A.
Tel. 800-637-2852
Fax 414-774-3259

AMADEUS PRESS
2 Station Road
Swavesey
Cambridge, CB4 5QJ, U.K.
Tel. 01954-232959
Fax 01954-206040

E-mail: orders@amadeuspress.com
Website: www.amadeuspress.com

Printed in China

Library of Congress Cataloging-in-Publication Data

Montparker, Carol.
  Polly and the piano / by Carol Montparker.
    p. cm.
  Summary: After being adopted from a shelter, Polly becomes a very good friend to her owner, who plays piano, gives lessons, and relies on Polly as she practices for and performs a very special concert.
  ISBN 1-57467-093-X
  1. Dogs--Juvenile fiction. [1. Dogs--Fiction. 2. Piano--Fiction. 3. Concerts--Fiction.]  I. Title.

PZ10.3.M697Po 2004
[E]--dc22
                                    2004018842

Visit our website at www.amadeuspress.com

*For Rollie, Zoe, Steven,*
*Linda, Julia, Maggie,*
*Bridey, and Lulu*

I am a black and tan puppy who waited a long time in the dog shelter for someone to adopt me.

One day a nice lady stopped in front of my cage, P.8.  She started singing a tune, and I cocked my head to listen, because I love music. I tried not to look too excited, but, oh, I hoped she would adopt me.

When the woman walked away quickly, I was so sad.  But then she returned with the keeper of the keys. He unlocked my cage, took me out, and handed me over to the lady named Laurel.

She named me Polly-Esther—(Polly for short), because I am a blend of breeds, and not a purebred dog.  She gave me a new green collar, and when we went into the house, there was a nice basket lined with a fuzzy, rose-colored pillow.

The basket was placed underneath a big black thing called a PIANO. It was so cozy that I curled up and went to sleep in my new home.

Every morning I awoke
and looked up to see a
strange roof over my
head, with wood and
brass parts.
It was the bottom of the piano.

When Laurel played the black and white
keys, wonderful vibrations went all
through me.
Laurel was a pianist and teacher, and
she used the piano a lot.

I had the most unusual doghouse
in the world.

Each week I waited for Laurel's students to come for their lessons. I loved to greet them, and they seemed to love me too.

My tail wagged like Laurel's metronome. I gave
each student a kiss on the hand and settled under
the piano to listen to the lesson. I learned Bach,
Mozart, Beethoven, Brahms, Chopin, and many
other great composers.

Sometimes when I loved the music, I couldn't help it . . .
I had to sing along.  I think it's because my ancestors were
wolves and liked to howl.

When I didn't like the music, I left my basket and went to lie far away from the piano.

My most special times were when Laurel
practiced for a concert and I could snuggl[e]
in very near the pedals.

Laurel would kick off her shoes and put her feet on my fur as she played. Even wh[en]
she is working hard, I feel she is connected to me, and knows I am here with her.
Laurel said, "Polly, you keep me from feeling lonely."

When Laurel
practiced too long,
I came and put
my muzzle and paws
on her lap, to tell
her to take time off.

"Okay, Polly,"
Laurel said. "Now
I'll play with you."

My favorite game is tug-of-war.
Laurel said, "Polly, I am afraid to pull your teeth out!"
But I am very strong, and I always win.

Even though I love my own bed under the piano, sometimes I like to play hide-and-seek among the stuffed animals on a bed upstairs.

On hot summer days while Laurel gardens, I scratch
myself a fresh patch of cool earth and hide under the azaleas,
watching for squirrels to dare to come on our property.

One day a kitten wandered into our garden, and I had to behave myself. I hoped that Laurel would not adopt another animal, and she said, "Don't worry, Polly. The kitten is only visiting. You're the only pet for me."

Laurel and I love to rock together on the porch. Laurel talks quietly to me while she watches birds. She pats me gently and tells me, "I love you, Polly. You are my best friend."

Laurel asks me for my paw in several languages. "*Donnes la patte*, Polly," she says in French, and I always understand.

Laurel tells me all her secrets, and one day she told me her dream to play the piano in Carnegie Hall.

Laurel practiced pieces by Mozart, Schubert, Chopin, and Ravel extra hard for her concert at Carnegie Hall. I never disturbed her, but pretended to be the critic from *The New York Times*. I barked or growled if I heard any wrong notes.

But when she played well, I went to the piano and licked her hand and wagged my tail.

One day I started feeling sad. Playing the piano seemed such a wonderful thing to do, that I wanted to try it too.

But how could I if I had paws instead of fingers?

All day long I dreamed about the piano and the stage. Laurel was trying to think of things to make me happy again.

Suddenly, Laurel said what I wanted to hear.
"I have a wonderful idea, Polly! Come over
to the piano. Would you like to try to play?"
I felt my tail wag a little.

I sat up on my hind legs on the piano bench and put my paws on the keys. When I pushed my paws down, funny sounds came out.

Laurel hugged me and said, "Polly, it seems you can only play modern music!" I didn't feel sad anymore.

Laurel said, "If everyone played the piano, who would be left to listen? You are my best listener, Polly. I am going to take you to Carnegie Hall with me so I don't feel so lonely on the stage."

I fell asleep listening to Laurel practice,
and dreaming of the big day.

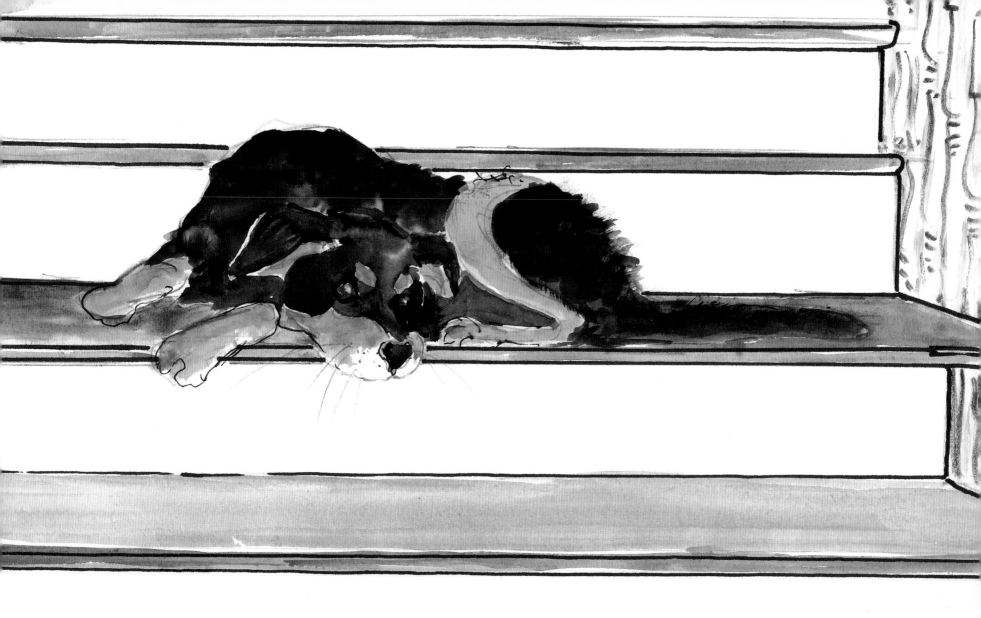

When the big day arrived, I waited and waited for Laurel
to get dressed so we could leave.

Our first glimpse of the great concert hall was from our ca
Laurel told me she was very excited and very nervous.

As we entered the front doors of Carnegie Hall, we paused to look at the poster announcing "Tonight's Concert." There was a big photo of Laurel behind a glass case.

Then we went backstage to wait for the moment when we had to walk out onto the stage.

Laurel said, "I don't know if I could do this without you, Polly."

There was a storm of applause when we entered the stage. Everything had a rosy glow to it. We did not look at the sea of faces, but walked straight to the huge black piano. Then I took my place quietly underneath, where I always sat when Laurel practiced. We were like partners.

Laurel played so beautifully, and while she played, I watched a thousand people listening to her. They were absolutely quiet, except for two people who coughed.

At the end of the concert, Laurel got many bouquets of flowers.
She took one big flower out of the bunch and gave it to me, saying,
"This is for you, Polly, the best music lover and friend in the whole world."

The End

The enclosed CD, composed of live performances by Carol Montparker, represents the concert that Polly heard being practiced and performed.

1–3. **Mozart**—Sonata in D, K. 576:
          Allegro (3:50)
          Adagio (4:55)
          Allegretto (4:26)

4–5. **Schubert**—Klavierstück in E-flat, D. 946, No. 2 (6:21)
          Impromptu in B-flat, Op. 142, No. 3 (9:59)

6–8. **Chopin**—Etude in F Minor, Op. 25 (1:34)
          Nouvelle Etude in F Minor (2:17)
          Ballade No. 4 in F Minor, Op. 52 (10:53)

9–11. **Ravel**—Sonatine:
          Modéré (4:29)
          Mouvement de Menuet (3:11)
          Animé (4:01)

Total Time 55:54

Recording Engineer: Norman Greenspan
CD Mastering: Clare Cerullo